D1417997

Jeanine Wine still considers herself a Chicagoan, although she now lives in Lancaster, Pa. She has illustrated two previous books, *Gladdys Makes Peace* and *Mattie Loves All.* This is the first book she has written.

Juv
PZ
7
.W7248
Mr
1987

MRS. TIBBLES and the Special Someone

Written and illustrated by Jeanine Wine

Intercourse, Pennsylvania 17534

C.I.P. data may be found on page 32
Copyright © 1987 by Good Books, Intercourse, PA 17534

GOSHEN COLLEGE LIBRARY
GOSHEN, INDIANA

Mrs. Tibbles worked in a big department store.

She sold shoes!

Every day she would run back and forth helping shoppers find shoes that fit.

By the end of the day her feet were very tired. In fact, they really hurt!

One evening, just as Mrs. Tibbles was getting ready to go home, the boss came to speak with her.

"Mrs. Tibbles," she said. "Get a lot of rest tonight because a very special person will be in the store tomorrow!"

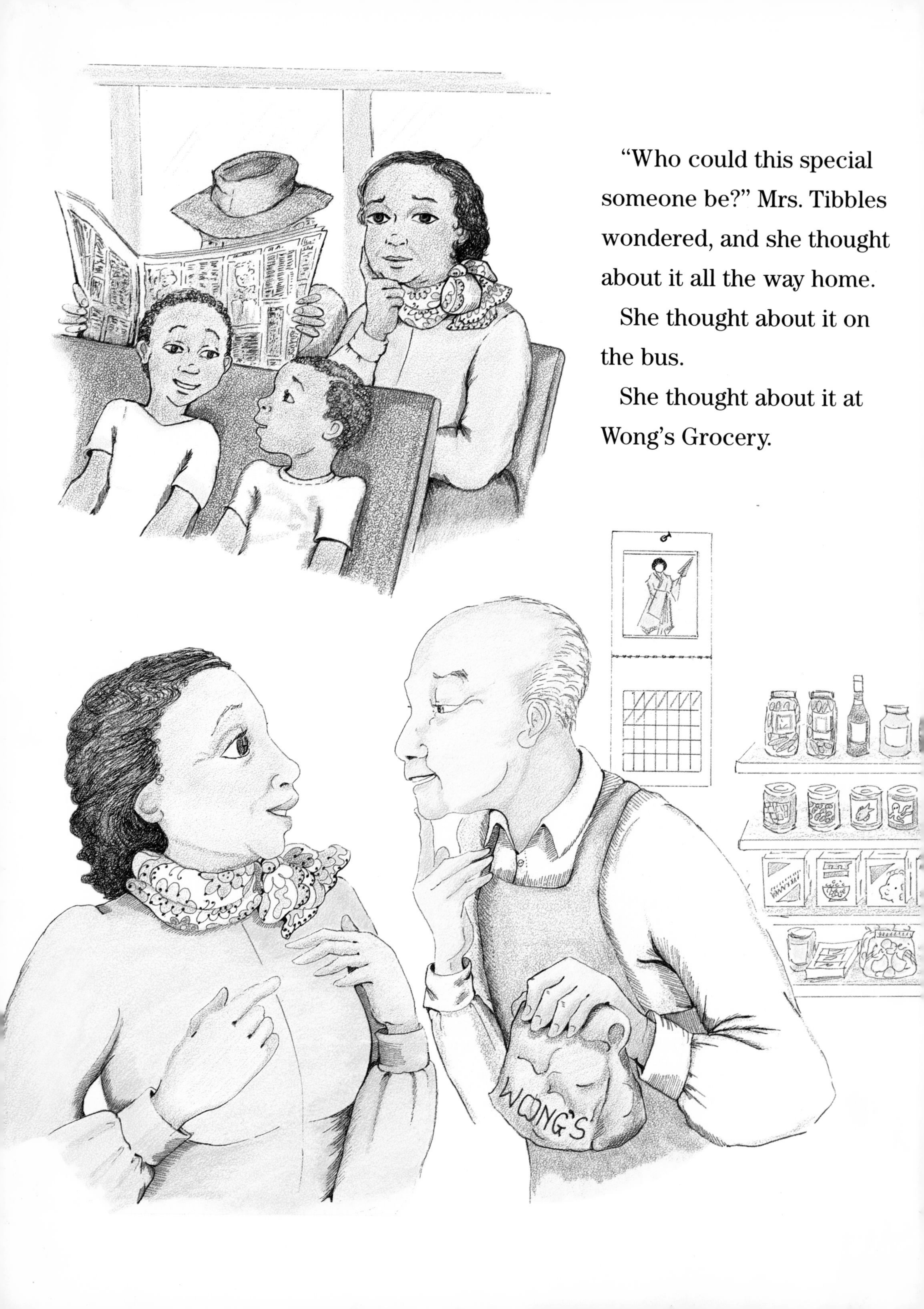

"Who could this special someone be?" Mrs. Tibbles wondered, and she thought about it all the way home.

She thought about it on the bus.

She thought about it at Wong's Grocery.

She thought about it as she greeted her landlady who owned the bakery over which Mrs. Tibbles lived.

“Maria,” she said, “someone special is coming to the store tomorrow. I wonder who it will be?”

Yesterday's rice casserole and Mr. Wong's egg rolls tasted especially good at dinnertime. Keesha's purring made Mrs. Tibbles so drowsy it was hard to stay awake.

When Mrs. Tibbles opened her eyes it was morning. She remembered what her boss had told her. Would someone special really be in the store today?

When she got to work she noticed a new man behind the jewelry counter.

She said, "Nice to work with you. My name is Mrs. Tibbles!"

The man just looked down his nose at her. You see, HE sold DIAMONDS and RUBIES and PRECIOUS STONES, and Mrs. Tibbles only sold shoes.

"Could this important man be the special person?" she thought.

Mrs. Tibbles went over to the shoe department. The store opened, and a big, shiny limousine pulled up in front of the window. A man got out of the car, opened the back door, and announced, "King William the Great here to visit the Grand Department Store."

Mrs. Tibbles watched as a dignified man with silver hair and many ribbons and medals on his coat climbed out of the car and came into the store.

GOSHEN COLLEGE LIBRARY
GOSHEN, INDIANA

King William walked right past Mrs. Tibbles, nodding his head in her direction, just a little.

Mrs. Tibbles was left only with the strong smell of his after-shave lotion. She wondered if that grand and powerful man was the special someone?

The day was very long with many customers trying on pair after pair of shoes.

A lady who looked like a movie star, walked up to Mrs. Tibbles and asked to be waited on. Someone even came up and asked the woman for her autograph. She had to be famous!

The woman tried on pair after pair of shoes and spent over three hundred and seventy-five dollars in the shoe department alone!

“I wonder if that famous and wealthy woman is the special person?” Mrs. Tibbles thought.

That night after closing time, Mrs. Tibbles was in the shoe department rubbing her aching feet.

All of a sudden a new janitor came by. Mr. Smith was his name.

“Ma’am” he said, “You look tired. I know just the thing for you!”

He went away for a little bit, then came back with a big tub of warm water for Mrs. Tibbles' feet.

The soothing water wrapped around her toes and lapped against her ankles. Aches and worries seemed to melt away. She felt just fine.

Keesha was peeping out the window, waiting for Mrs. Tibbles to come home.

As they shared a snack, Keesha heard about the people in the store that day.

"Who was the special someone?" Mrs. Tibbles wondered.

Keesha rubbed her fluffy back against Mrs. Tibbles' feet and they both knew right away!

Right then Mrs. Tibbles made up her mind to be a special someone too.

When a child trying on shoes started crying, Mrs. Tibbles would make a rabbit puppet out of a hankie and say, "There, there, it isn't so bad."

Or when a friend like Mrs. Wong was sick, Mrs. Tibbles would take chicken soup and a card.

And Mrs. Tibbles tried to be more kind to the man who sold jewelry.

One day, after he had waited on countless customers who had all been in a hurry, and his feet were tired and sore, Mrs. Tibbles looked at him and smiled.

She got a big tub of warm water ready,

and a few minutes later,
right there behind the
diamonds and the rubies, he
let Mrs. Tibbles soak his feet.

Mrs. Tibbles and the Special Someone
Copyright © 1987 by Good Books, Intercourse, PA 17534

International Standard Book Number: 0-934672-54-7
Library of Congress Catalog Card Number: 87-14966

All rights reserved. Printed in the United States of America. No part of this book may be reproduced in any form or by any means, electronic or mechanical, including photocopying, recording or by information storage and retrieval system, without permission.

Library of Congress Cataloging-in-Publication Data

Wine, Jeanine M.
Mrs. Tibbles and the special someone.

Summary: Mrs. Tibbles' boss tells her that someone special will be coming to the department store where she sells shoes but doesn't tell her who it will be.

|1. Department stores—Fiction. 2. Conduct of life—Fiction| I. Title.
PZ7.W7248Mr 1987 |E| 87-14966
ISBN 0-934672-54-7

JUV
FIC
WINE, J
MRS.

DATE DUE

NOV 26 1987	SEP 27 1989	FEB 25 199	MAR 28 2000
DEC 13 1987	OCT 25 1989	1-27-94	FEB 05 2001
12-18-87	FEB 07 1990	MAR 30 199	FEB 02 2002
1/6/88	FEB 19 1990	MAR 07 1995	FEB 15 2002
FEB 4 1988	MAR 05 1990	MAR 08 1995	MAR 10 2003
2/4/88	MAR 29 1990	MAR 29 1995	OCT 07 2012
MAR 19 1988	APR 04 1990	FEB 26 1996	
MAY 24 1988	FEB 04 1991	OCT 09 1996	
OCT 4 1988	MAR 03 1991	JAN 23 1997	
OCT 12 1988	APR 17 1991	FEB 24	
NOV 15 1988	9/2/91	APR 18 1997	
DEC 07 1988	9/19/91	NOV 25 1997	
JAN 25 1989	OCT 24 1991	FEB 09 1998	
JAN 31 1989	3-30-92	MAR 09 1998	
FEB 22 1989	9/19/92	APR 06 1998	
MAR 13 1989	11/9/92	APR 29 1998	
APR 10 1989	JAN 29 1993	APR 09 1999	
JUN 15 1989	FEB 13 1993		

GAYLORD PRINTED IN U.S.A.